VOLLEYBALL VIXENS: BRAZILIAN BOMBSHELLS

RILEY ROSE

BOOK 1 IN THE VOLLEYBALL VIXENS SERIES

A STORY IN THE DECADENT FANTASY UNIVERSE

Copyright

Copyright © 2022 Riley Rose

All rights reserved. No part of this publication may be reproduced, distributed, or transmitted in any form or by any means without the the prior written permission of the author, except in the case of brief quotations for review purposes.

This is a work of fiction and any resemblance to real people, places, or situations is coincidental.

Sign-Up for my E-Mail List to get a Free Ebook and to Stay Up-To-Date on Upcoming Books!

Visit RileyRoseErotica.com for more sexy stories!

Chapter 1

I leaped into the air, my long, dark brown hair whipping behind me, the sun gleaming on my scantily clad body.

This was my favorite moment. When time stood still and the whole world seemed to come into focus.

I exhaled and my hand smashed into the spinning ball, spiking it past my opponent's outstretched hands and sending it skipping off the silky sand.

"Yes!!" I screamed, raising my arms in triumph.

A familiar cry of glee greeted me as my sexy teammate hurtled toward me.

I jumped up, wrapping my arms and legs around her. Casey spun me around, and we hooted and hollered like total goofballs. But c'mon, we're totally entitled to be excited. We just won our first Futures Beach Tournament. And winning was so sweet!

Casey set me down and patted my bikini-clad butt several times while I returned her admiration with a few slaps to her shapely thigh. As beach volleyball partners, we had our hands over each other all the time. There was no one who knew my body more intimately than Case. Well, except for any cute girls I had sex with.

Speaking of which, there were two ridiculously cute girls we needed to go shake hands with: the Brazilian beauties we just defeated.

Actually, screw shaking hands. I was totally a hugger. I ducked under the net and embraced Carina, the shorter of the sexy duo. Her tanned, taut body pressed against mine as she wrapped her arms around my back and then gave me a nice slap on the ass. So nice it made me utter a cute yelp.

"You're a great player," she said in English with a super-sexy accent.

My hands lingered on her longer than a usual post-match embrace. "Oh, thanks. You're amazing! Um, I mean your playing, not um…" Ugh, why was I always so awkward? Like she really would have thought I was talking about her ridiculously hot body and not her beach skills.

She smiled and slapped my thighs. "See you soon sexy."

I inhaled sharply. Holy shit, was she flirting with me? Was my super-awkwardness actually attracting girls? Damn, I hoped so, because she was so pretty, and I totally admired her prowess on the court. And fuck that bikini looked so hot on her. The way it barely contained her supple booty within her swishing hips made me very wet.

Before I could continue my dorky flirting, we switched partners. Carina hugged Casey while Isabella wrapped me in a bear hug. These Brazilians were wonderfully affectionate. Izzie was the team's blocker and towered over me at 6'2". I was 5'8" (or 173 centimeters for everyone in the world besides us weird Americans) and one of the shorter players on tour, even though I was taller than your average non-volleyball-playing woman.

Isabella's arms were pure muscle, and she also seemed to have a penchant for my ass, patting it several times. My booty was apparently a big hit today.

After shaking hands with the officials and thanking them, Casey and I embraced again and jumped around like two giddy goofballs. I'm sure our barely covered butts were jiggling like crazy. But I didn't care. I was over the moon at winning our first tournament. This meant we could go on to the Challenge events, the middle tier on the Pro Tour. It was a huge step up for us and meant we were totally on our way to dominating the beach volleyball scene. Dominating in the nicest way possible. I really loved all the girls on tour.

The court announcer's voice boomed out in Spanish: "Your Tlaxcala winners, from the USA, Casey Chen and Alena Araya!"

We ran back out on court, waving to the crowd in the Plaza de Toros, one of the most unique and coolest places we had ever played. It was an old bullfighting arena from the 19th century with a 16th century Franciscan convent bell tower looming over it. The vibrant reds of the arena juxtaposed wonderfully against the older stone buildings of the former convent. It was a super-cool place to play, and I hoped the tour kept coming back here.

Casey and I answered the announcer's questions in English, and then I switched to Spanish, thanking the crowd for their awesome support. I think I won over some of the Mexican attendees with my flawless Spanish. My Chilean mom made sure I learned both it and English from the time I said my first words.

Casey only knew a little Spanish but was an expert in Thai, her dad hailing from Thailand. That's one reason we bonded so quickly our freshmen year at UCLA. We were both multi-racial, with one parent not originally from America. Plus we both loved volleyball and a ton of the same movies and shows. We had been best friends ever since and now, a year out of college, we've been trying to make it on the beach pro scene.

After the amazing medal ceremonies, we waved to the crowd one last time and retrieved our bags and water bottles.

Case slapped my butt as I bent over to retrieve my gear. "Leenie, you were amazing out there!"

I smiled and hugged her. That was her cute nickname for me. She was the only one who called me that, which made it even more special.

"Me? C'mon, you were a blocking machine. You're so fucking good!"

"I am, aren't I?" she replied with a grin. "Okay, we're both amazing!"

We laughed and hugged again.

"By the way, how much longer are you going to eye fuck Carina?"

Water sputtered out of my mouth and nose. "Wh... what? I... I'm not eye fucking her."

"Oh please, you're been ogling her hot ass the whole time."

Dammit, I didn't realize I had been that obvious. Of course, I never could keep anything from Casey.

"Th... that's only because she spanked me so hard and called me sexy."

"Oo, she called you sexy, huh?"

"No! I mean, um, maybe. It probably didn't mean anything."

"Of course it means something you dummy! It means she wants to eat your adorable pussy."

I blushed. How did she know it was adorable? Oh right, she had seen me naked on countless occasions when we changed into our bikinis or tried on new ones. Well, it was sweet she thought my pussy was so cute. I did keep my body in tip top shape. My stomach, arms, and legs were very toned. My butt both juicy and firm, at least that's what Casey said. And I had very perky breasts. They weren't huge, but they were a little larger than most girls on tour. A typical female volleyball player had a tiny chest, a ridiculously sculpted body, and an ass to die for. Which is why I was probably always so horny whenever I played. Especially the Brazilians, who were infamous for having the hottest asses on tour.

My lovable partner was no slouch in the hotness department either. She was 5'11", which believe it or not was undersized for a blocker, and her lean body was a temple to athletic perfection. Her boobs were smaller than mine, but her ass was chiseled like a Greek statue, and her arms and legs had the perfect amount of muscles to look both strong and sexy. It was easy to fantasize about her using those muscles to pin you down and fuck your brains out. Um, not that I ever had those kinds of fantasies.

"Do you really think so?" I asked, my crotch moistening at the thought of some epic Brazilian pussy licking.

"Only one way to find out!" She shoved me right into Carina, who was walking by us with her gear slung over her shoulder.

The Brazilian's sexy arms wrapped around me and prevented me from eating sand.

I clutched her, loving how close we were, intoxicated by her scent. Wait, how did she smell so nice after a three-set match? And oh shit, was I all stinky? Well, she wasn't pushing me away, so that was good.

"Oh, s… sorry Carina. Are you okay?"

"*Claro*. I'm never upset when a beautiful girl falls into my arms."

Ohhhh shit. That might have been the best line anyone had ever used on me. I swooned, and I would have fallen again if she didn't grab me more tightly.

"Alena," she said worriedly. "Are you feeling woozy? Do you want the trainer to check you out?"

"Oh, n… no, I'm fine," I replied. My cheeks were burning with embarrassment. How the heck could Carina like someone as dorky as me? "I think I'm just a little giddy from all the adrenaline."

She held onto me, making sure I could stand on my own. Over her shoulder, Casey and Isabella were smirking at us. Stupid Casey. I mean, not that stupid, because I did have a Brazilian beauty holding me tenderly.

Carina brushed some strands out of my face and smiled.

"Good. I want you at a hundred percent for our rematch. We're going to get you next time."

"You're on!" I replied. I would happily play her and Isabella every match, especially if they wore the string bikinis they currently had on, their tan, supple thighs on full display and making me think very naughty thoughts.

"Actually, Casey and I were wondering if you wanted to see the sights with us tomorrow. We're spending an extra couple of days to see Mexico City." The capital was two hours west of Tlaxcala. Case and I always liked to spend some extra time in the countries we visited to absorb some of the local custom. Traveling all over the world was one of the best things about playing beach volleyball. That and doing it with my best friend. Oh, and all the gorgeous hard bodies I was constantly around.

"We would love to *linda*, but we fly out early *manha*."

"Oh." My cheeks flushed. She just called me beautiful. It was nice when Spanish lined up with Portuguese. Geez, she was so nice. And so freakin' cute. "Y… you're so sweet."

Casey was now grinning ear to ear. She was going to tease me mercilessly later.

Carina turned to Isabella and spoke rapidly in their language.

Then her beautiful brown eyes gazed upon me again. "Tell you what. Meet us back here tonight. Say, nine?"

I tried to suppress a shiver. Was she asking us on a double date?

"Why back here?"

She smiled sensually. "You'll see."

I gulped. "O… okay. Um, that cool with you Case?"

"Hell yeah!" my trouble-making partner replied.

"Great! See you then." Carina patted my hips and sauntered off.

Isabella gave me a knowing smile as she followed. "*Tchau amigas.*"

"Bye." I waved awkwardly.

Casey wrapped her arms around me from behind. "See? I told you this pussy was getting fucked!" She patted the front of my swimsuit.

"Casey!" I scanned the stands. Everyone was filing out. So I guess no one was staring at us, but geez, couldn't she wait till we were in private to grope me.

"Oh c'mon, I totally just set you up with that gorgeous Brazilian. And maybe Isabella and I can have some fun too!"

"Aha! I knew you liked her."

"I'm not denying it. I'm just not all awkward about it like you."

"I am not… okay, fine I'm totally awkward. Please help!"

She giggled. "You don't need any help Leenie. It's why girls fall for you all the time."

I stared at her. They did? That was news to me.

"That and your world-famous ass." She smacked said posterior again.

"Hey!" How many people were going to fondle my butt today? And it was totally not world-famous. Was it? I mean, it's not like they were going to take a mold of it and put it in the Museum of Super-Hot Asses. Though if that place existed, I would get a lifetime membership.

"Guess what?" I said, taking my mind off hot asses for a moment. "We just won our first big tournament as pros!"

"Hell yeah we did!"

We clutched each other and did our happy dance, jumping up and down in a circle.

And then we finally skedaddled, high-fiving all the tournament staff on our way out.

Though I couldn't wait to return later tonight.

Chapter 2

We were on a natural high all the way back to the hotel. This is why I loved volleyball. There was no better feeling than winning a hard fought match. Well, except maybe sex with a super-cute Brazilian. Wait, was I going to have sex with her tonight? Okay, I was getting way ahead of myself. They probably just wanted to hang out as friends. Friends who liked fucking! *Ah! Alena stop it.* I needed to get my mind off my pussy.

We showered and changed into other bikinis, slipping T-shirts and shorts over them. Casey convinced me to wear one of my more revealing suits. She was a very bad influence. Though I didn't need much prodding, hoping Carina would think I looked sexy.

We chowed down and headed back to the venue, excited for our nighttime rendezvous.

The arena was deserted and looked a little eerie in the dark.

"Where do you think they are?" I asked, wrapping my arms around me.

Casey embraced me, making me feel better. "Don't worry. I'm sure they'll be here any minute. And if any criminals show up, Super-Casey will protect you!"

She stood with her hands on her hips in a classic Wonder Woman pose.

I giggled. "More like Super-Weirdo."

"Weirdos can be heroes too!"

I laughed harder and slipped my arm around her waist, going

up on my toes to kiss her on the cheek. "I love you Case."

She pecked me on the head. "Love you too Leenie."

"*Boa noite amigas,*" a pleasant voice greeted us.

Isabella smiled as she approached, Carina right behind her.

"Hey girls!" the shorter Brazilian greeted us. Though at 5'9" she still had an inch on me.

"Hey you two!" Casey replied as I waved.

"So, about that rematch?" Carina had a gleam in her eye. Uh oh, I had found another troublemaker.

"What about it?" my partner asked.

"How about right now?" Her eyes flicked to the darkened arena.

"But they must have locked it," I protested.

"Izzie is very convincing." Carina looked at her friend, who smiled and held up a set of keys.

I gaped at the silver gleaming in the moonlight. Damn, these girls had lots of handy skills. I hoped they would have their hands all over us soon. Shit. I was doing it again. But c'mon, they were so hot! Their skin was so tan and flawless. Their faces so cute. Their bodies so perfectly sexy and athletic.

I sighed. Yup, I had it bad.

"Let's go!" Casey proclaimed. She was always eager to break the rules.

"Um, won't we get in trouble?"

"It's fine," Carina replied, hooking her arm in mine. "They're not taking things down until *manha*. So it's all ours tonight."

"What are we waiting for?" Casey snatched Isabella's hand and yanked her toward the entrance.

Carina followed suit, pulling me along. Her hand was soft, even with some of the callouses that came from playing. A thrill shot through me. Both from our illicit activity and her touch.

Isabella unlocked the gate and we scampered inside, locking it behind us.

The court was still set up. Though it looked strange with no lights on inside an empty stadium.

Carina plucked a ball out of her bag and tossed it to me.

I caught it with both hands, rotating the familiar yellow, blue, and white orb. I would happily give them a rematch, especially if it meant seeing their gorgeous bodies in skimpy bikinis again. They were wearing shorts and tank tops, but I knew they had something scandalous on underneath.

"So, normal rules?" I asked.

"Yes, but with a twist," Carina replied with a devilish smile.

The stadium lights blared on, and Isabella reemerged. I didn't even see her leave. That one was sneaky!

"Oo, we love twists," Casey commented. I was about to tell her to speak for herself, but I was intrigued at what our Brazilian friends had in store.

"If you lose a set," the lovely Carina continued. "You have to strip and play the next set naked."

"What?!" My mouth hung open, wondering if I had heard her correctly.

"You're on!" Casey eagerly agreed.

"Case!"

"What?"

"What the hell are you doing?"

"Um, agreeing to a sexy match with two beautiful Brazilians."

"Yeah, but..." I sputtered. Okay, when she put it like that, it seemed silly to protest.

"C'mon Alena, wouldn't you like to see more of this?" Carina took her top off and slid her shorts down. Ohh man, that was a tiny bikini. Even skimpier than the one she wore during our match earlier today.

Isabella followed suit, and there were now two beautiful women standing before us, wearing practically nothing.

My mouth dropped again. I think I may have been drooling. I so wanted to see more of that.

"We will totally dominate your hot bodies!" I announced. "Oops, I mean on the court." I blushed, not intending to say all that out loud.

Carina smiled, evidently enjoying how goofy I was. Maybe Casey was right about that being part of my charm. Who knew?

"*Tira as tuas roupas,*" Isabella said in a commanding tone.

"Um, what?" She was pointing at our pussies. Holy shit, did they want to go straight to sex and skip the match?

"She wants you to strip," Carina translated.

"Hey we haven't lost yet," I protested.

"No *boba*, just to your sexy bikinis."

"Oh right. O... okay." I don't know why I was hesitant. I played in front of huge crowds in a bikini all the time. But the fact that I might soon be playing stark naked if we lost made me more shy than usual.

Luckily, I had a very non-shy goofball of a friend. Casey yanked my shirt off and then tackled me to the sand, where she proceeded to unzip my shorts and whisk them down my shapely legs.

I wound up on my stomach, which meant my ass was on full display for the Brazilian girls. Casey whacked it, my well-tanned flesh jiggling provocatively.

"Ah Case!"

"I love your bottoms Alena," Carina gushed.

I stayed on my stomach, letting her ogle me some more. Casey and I had chosen more risque bikinis for this illicit rendezvous.

They weren't thongs but they did reveal generous portions of our asses, especially on me. I had a curvier butt than Case, which according to her, made everyone wet when I shook it. I didn't try to shake it all sexy like. That's just how my hips moved. But if my somewhat naked posterior was turning Carina and Isabella on, I would shake it for all it was worth.

I was going to tear Casey's clothes off to get her back for her sneaky strip attack, but she already disrobed, showing off her athletic body in a matching swimsuit.

I stuck my tongue out at her as she helped me to my feet. "You suck."

She smiled and hugged me. "Love you too Leenie!" Ugh, I could never stay mad at her. She was too adorable.

"*Vamos jogar!*" Isabella beckoned.

I watched her and Carina walk to one side of the court. And that's when I got my first view of the back of their bikinis: they were wearing skimpy thongs, their hot, curvy, tone asses undulating in the most sensual way possible.

"Ohhh God," I cooed, mesmerized by the Brazilian booties shaking back and forth.

"Hey no fair!" Casey added. "You're trying to distract us with your super-hot asses."

"Like you aren't?" Carina replied with a smirk.

I sighed. Okay, we kind of were with our suit choice.

"Dammmit, I knew we should have gone with the thongs," Casey said.

I took her hands. "Listen, we can do this. Just stay focused and play like we did earlier today."

"Right. And getting to see those chicks naked is a great motivator!"

I giggled. "It totally is!"

We hugged and slapped each other's thighs, then ran to the

other side of the court.

Carina informed us the players wearing the skimpiest bikinis always got to serve first, and we really couldn't argue with that. Casey and I got into our defensive positions, hands on our knees, each taking a half of the court.

Isabella stood by the net, getting ready to block, while Carina spun the ball in her hands, deciding who she wanted to serve to.

She tossed the colorful orb in the air, jumped, and whacked it with her right hand.

It just cleared the net and swerved to the right. I dove with outstretched arms, digging it just before it hit the sand. Ah, she was being all tricky right off the bat. We'd see about that you super-sexy sneaky server.

Casey was in perfect position, bump setting the ball high and several inches off the net.

I scurried to my feet, propelled myself off the soft sand, and whacked the ball hard. It ricocheted off Isabella's outstretched hands, but luckily fell on their side of the court.

"Yeah!!" I yelled, pumping my fist and double high-fiving Casey.

"Great shot Leenie!" She slapped my thigh and went back to serve, catching the ball from Isabella.

I set up in the backcourt, bending over and holding my hands behind my butt, sticking my index finger out on both hands. This was super-secret volleyball code. Casey liked to say the number of fingers girls held up meant how many digits they wanted stuck in their tight pussies. But she's a raging nymphomaniac so don't listen to her. Though I might sometimes fantasize about our opponents slipping their hands down the front of my bottoms and exploring my depths. Hmm, maybe Casey was on to something after all.

Okay, but here's the real deal on the signals. Flashing one

finger meant I wanted Case to block the lines while I covered any cross court shots from our cute opponents. If I gave her two fingers, it was the opposite: she'd block angle shots and I'd watch for blasts down the sidelines. Basically it meant Casey and I spent a lot of time staring at each other's butts. Which wasn't a bad thing. Hers was really cute!

Case's serve whizzed over the net. Carina dug it, passing it to Isabella who overhand set it perfectly back to her partner.

The cute Carina blasted a spike past Casey's block. I dove, stabbing out one hand. It bounced off my wrist, careening out of bounds.

Casey sprinted past me and performed an amazing Superman dive, flicking it back toward me. I scrambled up and bumped it high over the net, giving Casey time to get back in position.

Unfortunately, that gave Carina and Isabella a total free ball. And they put it to good use, utilizing a sneaky pokey to lift the ball over Casey's outstretched hands and just out of my reach, tying the game.

Casey helped me up, and we dusted the sand off our butts. I was about to pull down my bottoms, which had really ridden up my crack when Casey grabbed my hand.

"Leave it that way."

"What? Why?"

"Duh, so we can distract them more with your supernova ass."

"Supernova ass?"

"Yeah, when people look at it, it causes a supernova of orgasms."

I burst out laughing. That was the most ridiculous thing I had ever heard. But also kind of the nicest. Casey always made me feel good about myself. That's just one reason I loved her so much.

"You're the weirdest and most amazing best friend in the world."

"I know."

We giggled and brushed more sand off each other.

"What's so funny over there you two?" Carina asked.

"Oh sorry, I was just convincing Alena to show you more of her hot ass." She spun me around and spanked my much more exposed booty, shaking my cheeks.

Isabella said something to Carina in Portuguese. Then the shorter Brazilian called out to us. "You're an excellent influence Casey."

I wrinkled my nose. Sure, an excellent influence on getting me to show off my naughty bits. Of course, I wasn't making any effort to adjust my bikini. If our two lovely opponents liked looking at my bouncing butt that much, who was I to deny them. And okay, maybe I liked being naughty. But don't tell anyone because this naughty girl stuff is kind of new to me.

We continued the first set, filled with spikes, digs, cuttees, screams, and groans. We were all playing full out. Even though a championship wasn't on the line, something even more important was: our naked bodies!

It was 22-21 in favor of the Brazilians. Isabella was serving for set point. Oh, quick volleyball info time: you have to win by two in volleyball, so sometimes sets could go way beyond 21. See how much cool stuff you're learning!

Izzie rocketed the ball over the net. It smashed off my upper arms and chest. Damn, that girl served hard. I wonder if she liked to fuck hard too. Shit! I needed to focus.

The ball sprang off me, and Casey scrambled to it, bumping it toward the net.

I leaped forward, using my knuckles to deliver a soft pokey to the back of the court. Ha, Carina would never be able to run that down.

Except she did. She was like a ninja, a blur moving across the court and somehow digging the ball off the sand. Wow. I think I might be in love. She was so fucking good.

Isabella anticipated her teammates's amazing prowess and was in perfect position to bump the ball in a lovely set.

Carina ripped a sizzling spike past Casey's block and right in front of me, spitting up sand into my face.

The talented Brazilians hooted and hollered, hugging each other as they celebrated winning the first set.

Casey embraced me. "Don't worry babe. We'll get them in the next set."

Usually I shook off losing a set pretty easily. It was important to have a short-term memory and focus on winning the next one. But this wasn't a normal game.

I nodded. "Right. But… we… we have to…"

"Strip and show us those hot bodies!" Carina called as she and Isabella ducked under the net and approached us.

She and Izzie wore ridiculously huge grins.

"Do… do we have really have to get naked?"

"C'mon *minha fofinha*, we made a deal."

"Yeah Alena," Casey unhelpfully chimed in. "Show those sexy tits and ass!"

I put my hands on my hips, pouting. "You're getting naked too you know."

"Oh I know. I can't wait!"

I rolled my eyes. Casey had always been very comfortable with her body, having no problem being in the buff. I wished I had her confidence.

Carina clasped her hands together. "Please Alena, will you show us your gorgeous body?"

Isabella nodded along eagerly. They booth seemed very earnest about seeing my natural assets.

I blushed. Well, geez, if they were going to ask so nicely, how could I refuse? And we did make a deal. It was only right that I honor our agreement.

"O… okay."

"Yes!" All three of them said in unison.

I blushed a lot harder.

"Okay, tops first," Casey commanded. "At the same time."

I nodded. If I was going to show my girls, I wanted to do it while Casey was also revealing hers.

I tugged my tiny top over my head, my boobs bouncing gently as they came free.

I glanced at Casey. Her tits were standing at attention, small but ridiculously firm. And she was flaunting them, having no issue being half-naked.

Then I stole a peek at our friends/opponents. They licked their lips as they took in our multiple mounds.

"Oo Alena," Carina cooed. "I see stripping gets you excited."

"What?" I looked down. My nipples were protruding, hardening into very sensitive nubs. Stupid nips.

"I… I just…"

Casey squeezed my tits. "Oh Alena is crazy horny!"

"Casey!" What the hell? She was fondling me and revealing all my sexy secrets. Of course, I wasn't moving her hands away from my mini-mountains.

"It's always the good girls that are," Carina teased.

I sighed. What was this, make fun of Alena day? I could be a good girl and still be horny. Especially when surrounded by gorgeous, half-naked women.

"Oh, can we just finish getting naked?"

"Yes ma'am!" Case eagerly agreed. "Let's get these skimpy bottoms off."

Before I could yank my bikini down, Casey stopped me. "No silly, turn around."

"What? Why?"

"Duh, to show them both your ass and pussy when you strip. And be sure to do it all slow-like."

I gaped at her. Had she been a stripper in a previous life? How was she so good at this?

Carina and Izzie jumped up and down. "Yes! Definitely do that." Isabela echoed Carina in Portuguese. One thing I had to say: these two ladies were very eager to see us naked. It was quite flattering actually.

I turned around, following my sexy, weird friend's lead. I bent forward, slipping my fingers under the soft fabric of my bikini bottoms and slowly tugging them down.

I revealed my ass an inch at a time, feeling extremely naughty. And then my pussy lips sprang free, eliciting a gasp from the two lovely voyeurs. That inspired me to present them with a little booty shake as I pushed my bottoms farther down, staying bent over longer than was needed, until I finally stepped out of the tiny garment.

I faced the Brazilian girls, holding my naked body and feeling very exposed.

Casey slapped my ass, making me drop my arms. "Stop covering up your super-hotness."

"Okay, okay, geez." Casey always had a fun way of making me feel all sexy. I presented my nudeness to our friends. They spent a long time taking in our nubile bodies.

"*Bonita*," Isabella gushed.

"So beautiful," Carina agreed, staring at me like she was in la la land.

I glanced down my body, trying to hide my reddening cheeks. Well, I guess I was kind of sexy. My tits were really perky. I had a smooth stomach with well-defined abs. My hips curved nicely around my ample booty. And my legs were long and toned. Oh and I guess my pussy was cute. At least Casey thought it was.

And apparently Carina and Izzie did too as they kept staring at it. And Casey's too of course. And her whole body. She was so fucking hot. She had the perfect combination of athleticism and sexiness. She possessed enough muscles to look like she should join The Avengers while still having sexy curves in all the right places. I wonder how many girls she held with those powerful muscles, making them cum like good little whores. Um, not that I fantasized about that. Because I totally didn't!

"This is going to be the best set ever!" Carina proclaimed.

I stuck my tongue out at her. "Sure, you're not the one who has to play naked."

"But I am the one who gets to watch." She gave me an impish grin, then ducked back under the net.

Casey sidled up beside me. "Wow, your flirting isn't as awkward as usual. Maybe you should get naked more often."

I shoved her. "You're so funny. Will you just go serve you naked nymph?"

"Naked nymph? Oo, I like that. I'll come up with a cute nude name for you too!"

"Gee, thanks."

"You're welcome!" She slapped my butt and ran back behind the end line. Oh! That felt different on totally bare skin. Usually I had at least a thin layer of swimsuit covering my cheeks when she spanked me. That felt... kinda nice.

I turned around, taking up a defensive position and flashing signals to Casey. It was so weird doing this in the nude. The wind caressed my bare pussy and made me shiver. Not because it was cold. It was actually a pleasantly warm night. But because I was getting turned on playing naughty volleyball. Hey, naughty volleyball - that was a great idea for a new sport. Everyone plays in the nude and then there's a big orgy at the end! Oh no! My horny brain was working overdrive thanks to these hot Brazilians and my goofy partner. Or maybe I was just excessively horny.

I waited for the sweet sound of Casey hitting the ball. But it didn't come.

I glanced back. "Um, Case, what are you waiting for?"

"Oh sorry. I got distracted staring at your hot, naked ass."

I rolled my eyes again. Oh boy. "Will you just serve you goofball!"

"Well excuse me for being obsessed with your world famous butt."

I couldn't hide my smile. Oh Casey. She was one in a million. I was glad she was my one in a million.

Naughty volleyball commenced, our naked bits bouncing all over the place, pointed out with glee in the running color commentary our rivals provided. Ugh, we totally had to win this set and get them just as naked as we were. This was so embarrassing. But also a total turn on.

What if I dived for the ball and Carina helped me up, ogling my sand-covered pussy. She could offer to help me clean if off, her fingers brushing my lips, then accidentally piercing my tightness. I gasp and seize up, her fingers navigating my tiny, intricate channel. Causing rapids to swirl inside me. Making me clutch her and beg her to go deeper. Beg her to own my ass, tits, and pussy. Oh fuck, she's so far in. She's about to hit my… ohhhhhh God yes! Yes! Yes! Yes!

Ow! The ball ricocheted off my face, toppling me onto my back and snapping me out of my sensual daydream.

Casey, Carina, and Izzie ran over, kneeling beside me.

"Leenie, are you okay?"

"I'm so sorry Alena. I would never aim at such a beautiful

face."

I blushed as they helped me sit up. Both from my illicit fantasy and Carina's lovely compliment.

"I'm fine," I replied, rubbing my sore cheek. "It was totally my fault. I was daydreaming."

"More like sex dreaming." Casey pried my legs apart, showing my wetness.

Oh my God! I clamped my thighs shut, shoving my obnoxious friend. "Casey!"

Carina and Izzie squeezed my thighs. "Oo Alena, you were fantasizing about us fucking you." It wasn't so much a question as a statement, like she completely understood my kinky mind. Damn that Carina was one smart, sexy lady.

"N... no. I totally wasn't dreaming about you fingering my tight pussy!" I clamped my mouth shut, not meaning to blurt that out.

Carina beamed at me, then translated for Isabella. And then she had just as big of a goofy grin.

I covered my face, wishing I could disappear. Man, playing naked really made it hard to hide your horniness.

Casey tore my hands down and smothered me in a hug. "I love you, you little slut!"

"Not helping Case."

She kissed me on the cheek and yanked me up. "C'mon, let's get these two naked and then maybe your fantasy can become a reality."

My cheeks reddened further. Oh boy, I would love that.

Carina gave me one of her sensual, impish grins. "Maybe indeed *bonita*."

She and Izzie scurried to the other side of the net, leaving me even wetter than before.

Casey glanced down my body. "Should I get a bucket to catch all the cum you're about to leak out?"

"Casey!" I chased her around the court, determined to get her back for her teasing. She just laughed and shook her butt, while the Brazilians enjoyed the show.

After I finally caught her and a tickle fight broke out, we realized we should probably get back to the game and stop giving our friends a free porn show.

Okay, back to a volleyball beatdown. After all our naked flaunting, I was even more determined to make these ladies strip.

We had another epic set. You might think it wouldn't be that weird playing in the buff since we didn't wear that much to begin with. But it was. I got sand up my ass crack and inside my pussy. Not to mention all over my tits and everywhere else.

But I guess it looked sexy as hell as Carina and Isabella kept ogling us between points.

My equally sand-coated friend ran up, handing me the ball. "Is it okay if I spank you?"

"Case, you spank me all the time." Ass slaps were a regular part of the game after all.

"I mean a lot more than usual. Since we're naked, the more we feel each other up and jiggle our naughty bits, the more we'll distract them."

"This is your great plan for victory?"

"Yes. It's an amazing plan. Haven't you been distracted by them? And they're still partially clothed."

Hmm, she had a point. And they definitely enjoyed watching me chase Casey around in the buff. "Okay, fine you can feel me up as much as you want."

"Yes! Oh, and you should slap my booty a bunch too."

"You just like getting spanked."

"Damn right. Almost as much as you do you little slut."

"Hey, I do not... ack!" My protest was cut off by a vicious ass slap.

Casey scurried to the net, leaving me rubbing my sore booty. And thinking about how good her attack felt. Shit, maybe I did love getting spanked. And maybe Carina could test just how much I loved it after the match. Oh wait, I wasn't supposed to be thinking of her hot body. I was supposed to be concentrating on winning. And then I could ogle her hot, naked body. Now that was some awesome motivation!

The rest of the set saw Casey fondling me all over. I was very used to and comfortable with her touching me all the time during matches. Female volleyball partners probably had the closest relationship outside of actual lovers. But geez, this was crazy! My ass got slapped, squeezed, and played with like it was her personal toy. Hey, I'm not saying I didn't enjoy it. I'm just saying, fuck this girl had grabby hands. Of course, I shouldn't talk. I tried to give it back to her as much as I got it, pinching and slapping her smaller but still super-cute booty.

And all our ass-grabbing apparently was working because we were up 20-15 and the Brazilian duo made some uncharacteristic mistakes. Yes! Our hot butts were totally defeating them. That's something I never thought I'd say in a match.

Casey handed the ball to me. "Let's make those sluts strip!"

"Right! But I actually think they're really nice girls."

"Of course they're nice. I'm just calling them sluts because I want to fuck them."

"Oh. Me too!" Oh shit. Did I say that out loud?

She grinned at me. "No kidding. I can tell from your bullet nips and drenched pussy."

I peered at my chest. Oh crap, when did they get that hard? Probably from all the spankings Casey had been giving me. And I think my lower lips had stayed saturated ever since my illicit daydream. Hey, being naked really turned me on, okay?

Well, it was time to deliver an ace and see some tasty Brazilian tits. They shouldn't get to have all the fun seeing us in the buff.

I scooped up some sand and let it fall. The wind blew it back toward me and to the left, letting me know how to adjust my serve.

I spun the ball a few times, picked my spot, and delivered a floater. Instead of the usual high-speed serve, this one was soft and dropped just over the net, ideally catching your opponent off guard.

It almost worked. But we had really good opponents. Carina dove, throwing her hand out and pancaked it, sending the ball straight up.

Isabella got another hand on it and then Carina had to awkwardly leap over her partner to slap it over the net.

It was an ugly hit, meant to keep the ball alive. I wasn't going to give our sexy opponents the chance to get back into position.

I gave it a solid whack and sent a rainbow over their heads to the back corner. They had no chance.

"Woohoo Alena!! You did it!"

Casey grabbed me around the waist and swung me in circles. I laughed and held on to her neck, letting her euphoria wash over me.

We jumped up and down holding each other after the spinning stopped.

"We're going to see hot Brazilian booties!" I gushed.

"Hell yeah! Brazilian booties! Brazilian booties!"

I joined in her chant, gazing at our beautiful opponents. Okay, so we were being juvenile. But c'mon, if you saw how hot these two were, you'd be doing a stupid dance too.

They approached us slowly. "Don't stop on our account," Carina said. "We're enjoying your tits and asses shaking all over."

Whoops. I forgot we were naked and putting on a sexy show for them. No wonder they didn't mind our hijinks.

"Well it's time for you to show us some T&A!" Casey announced.

"If, um, that's okay with you," I added politely.

Carina grinned. "Of course. You won fair and square. Though I expect the excessive groping was to throw us off our game."

"What? Of course not. Alena and I feel each other up like that all the time, even when we're not playing."

I whacked Casey's shoulder. "Casey!"

Then gazed at the object of my affection. "Um, well, after you and Izzie are all naked, you can totally try to distract us too."

She took a step closer, her breath tickling my nose. "You'd like that, wouldn't you?"

"Ohh God yes." I hadn't meant for that to come out so hot and desperate.

She spoke quickly to Isabella, who gave her and us two big thumbs up. Guess she was okay with the fondling distraction plan. Where we actually going to play the last set or just feel each other up? I was totally okay skipping right to the groping part.

Carina stepped back and put her arms over her head. Izzie hopped behind her and began untying her sexy bikini top.

Oh shit. They were going to strip each other. That was so much better than stripping on their own.

"We totally should have done that," I murmured to Casey, my eyes never leaving the Brazilian beauties before us.

"We have so much to learn," my teammate agreed.

Isabella slowly continued her untying, teasing us with her partner's perfect breasts. Okay, I hadn't seen them yet, so I didn't know they were perfect. But I had an uncanny ability to picture exactly what girls' boobs looked like underneath their swimsuits. I should totally be a superhero with that power.

Casey and I clutched each other, both getting wet at the anticipation.

Izzie finally gave us what we wanted, whisking Carina's top off. Oh yeah, those were perfect. Two exquisitely shaped petite breasts greeted us, inviting us to suck on their erect nipples and make love to them. Oh, did I mention I'm also fluent in tit talk? Perky nips could communicate a lot!

"Carina you're so gorgeous!" I exclaimed.

She gave me that radiant smile of hers. I would have melted into a puddle of goo on the floor if Casey wasn't holding me.

Carina switched places with Izzie and sexy striptease'd her friend's dual threats. They were a little smaller than Carina's but completely firm and tanned. These girls obviously sunbathed nude. They had so many awesome habits!

"Izzie you are hot stuff!" Casey announced with a helpful translation by Carina. Isabella grinned and squeezed her perky girls.

"Please show us your hot asses and pussies!" I yelled way too loudly.

That took everyone by surprise.

"Holy shit Alena," Casey commented. "I don't know if I've ever seen you this horny."

I bit my lip. "Oh, um, sorry. It's just… you two are so sexy and beautiful and…"

Casey pinched my sides and whispered into my ear. "You are crushing so bad."

I pinched her back. "Would you shush?"

The two Brazilians were amused by our antics. I was grateful they dug weird American girls.

Carina spun Isabella around and slipped her fingers underneath the sides of her bottoms.

Casey and I seized each other tighter. Yes! Here came the

really good stuff.

Carina slowly tugged Izzie's thong down, freeing it from her sculpted ass and yanking it down to her feet, where her friend stepped out of her unneeded garment.

Damn, that was one firm ass. I rotated Casey, comparing her muscular booty to Isabella's.

"Um, what are you doing?"

"Trying to figure out which of you has the tighter ass," I replied like that was a totally normal thing to do.

"Oh, okay." Casey was very good-natured about that kind of thing. "You're getting awfully frisky for a girl who supposedly didn't want to get naked."

I pinched and slapped her booty to shut her up. And, well, it helped me determine how hot it was.

"Hey! I mean, keep doing that."

I giggled. What a weirdo. A weirdo who I totally spanked again.

Carina did the same to Izzie, who suffered the spankings with equal delight as Casey.

"Let's switch," Carina suggested.

We swapped partners and felt up the muscular ass we weren't as familiar with. Izzie made cute noise as I squeezed her wonderful butt. Casey made even louder noises. She loved being vocal when being felt up.

"I believe they are equally firm and delicious," Carina declared.

"I agree. But it was very important we conducted that test." She and I giggled and touched each other's arms. Her hands were warm and soft. I wanted her to touch me a lot more.

"Okay you two," Casey interrupted. "It's time to compare your two scrumptious asses. Carina, strip!"

My breath caught. I had been excited to see Carina's bare

bottom and luscious lips since we made the nude bet.

She turned around, bent over, and slid her bottoms off right in front of me.

Oh. My. Fucking. God. I had a front row seat to the hottest ass and tastiest pussy I had ever seen. Her butt was an amazing blend of both firmness and suppleness. It was the perfect size. Not one of those tiny butts. One that was just right and that you could get both hands on, squeezing two hot cheeks.

And that pussy. Totally shaved. Totally cute. And totally needing my tongue inside it. If Carina was okay with that. I'm pretty sure she was based on how she was wiggling her butt in front of me.

When she turned around, I probably had the dorkiest expression on my face. But she wasn't looking at that. Her gaze fell between my legs.

I followed it and noticed not only my pussy was moist, but my inner thighs too. Oh God, I was even wetter than earlier. Her nakedness was too much for my tender pussy to take.

I crossed my legs, trying to hide my leaky faucet.

Carina was having none of that. She eased her leg between mine, separating my thighs. "Don't be embarrassed *meu chuchu*. It is very flattering."

"O… okay." The soft flesh of her leg rubbed against me, and I wanted nothing but to surrender myself to this Brazilian goddess. Besides her obvious beauty, she was kind and caring and totally my kind of girl.

"Now, let's test that world-famous ass of yours." She spun me around and seized my feisty bottom, making me gasp loudly. Oh fuck, she was an amazing ass grabber, her fingers kneading into my supple flesh like it was submissive butter. But wait, she called my booty world-famous too. Casey was the only one who teased me about that. Was my ass talked about that much on tour?

Maybe I could make the Hot Asses Volleyball Calendar. I don't think there was such a thing, but there totally should be. With Carina, Casey, and Izzie all on it!

After Carina felt up every ounce of my derrière, she let Isabella grab her booty while Casey immediately seized mine.

"Fuck Case!" I exclaimed as she squeezed me like she owned my butt.

"Carina wants you so bad," she whispered.

"Y… you really think so?" I sighed. Both from crushing on Carina and from Casey's soothing ass massage. After her initial attack, she relaxed into gently kneading my flesh. She actually had wonderfully nimble and soft fingers.

"Uh huh. Aren't you glad we decided to play naked volleyball?"

Ohhhh," I cooed. "Y… yeah, so glad." I leaned back against her. "Can you move down just a… oh yeah, that's it."

"You're very compliant when your butt is being felt up."

"Less teasing and more massaging you sexy weirdo."

I could feel her smile just from the way her body moved. We had become so close over the years we knew how the other would react even with our eyes closed. Which is why I always felt safe in Casey's arms. Especially when she was giving me an epic ass massage.

Isabella said something in Portuguese as she dutifully felt up her partner.

"She said both our butts would make everyone in the stands flood the stadium with cum if they saw us naked."

I blushed. Wow. Now that was a visual.

"So what she's saying is, you two should play all future matches in the buff," Case helpfully translated.

"That is not what she's saying you goofball."

"Goofball?" She squeezed hard, raising me up on my toes.

"Ahh! I mean super-nice, incredibly beautiful goofball."

She eased up. "That's better. But I agree, it's hard to determine who has the sexier ass. Should we just keep feeling you guys up for the next few hours?"

I was about to protest when I realized I was totally down with Carina and Casey having their way with my submissive butt for the rest of the night. I was becoming very naughty on this trip.

"I have a better idea," Carina said. "Whoever loses the third set has to become the sex toys of the winners."

Casey and I froze. Holy shit. Um, what?

Case grabbed me tightly around the waist. "Did she just say what I think she said?"

"Uh huh," I replied, holding onto her arms.

Carina and Izzie leaned against each other, posing provocatively. "What do you say *amigas*?"

Casey spun me around, clutching my forearms. "Can we please be fuck toys Leenie?"

I sighed. What a little nympho I had for a best friend. Of course, I was the one leaking my girl juices everywhere.

"No," I replied, which got me a frowny face from her. "Because we're going to win and be making the fuck toys. I mean they're going to be our... oh you know what I mean."

She hugged me. "I sure do! You're the best." She peered over my shoulder at our rivals. "You sluts are going down!"

Carina smiled. "We'll see who the true sluts are after the set." Oo, I liked her confidence. And quite frankly, it was really a win-win. Either we got to dominate them or they got to ravish us. Either way, there was lots of hot, naked rolling around in the sand in my near future. Fuck, I loved this game!

"Let's do this!" I proclaimed, my competitive juices firing back up. Hopefully, they would outweigh my pussy juices during the final set.

It was time to play the most important match of our lives.

Chapter 3

I had never been so focused on winning a set before. Okay, that's totally not true. I was also way too focused on Carina and Izzie's naked assets bouncing all over the place. How the heck was I supposed to concentrate with their hot tits and asses covered in sand like they were posing for some sexy photo shoot?

Of course, Casey and I were in a similar state. The set was so competitive we were constantly diving to dig balls and getting sand all over our bare bodies.

It was 13 all. Casey received the serve and passed it to me. I gave her a juicy set, spying our opponents as soon as I did.

"Line!" I screamed.

Casey blasted it down the left side, hitting the line.

"Yeaaaah!" She pumped her fist in celebration.

I ran over and gave her a super-hug. "Woohoo! Amazing shot Case!"

"One more point. You got this!"

Unlike the first two sets, the third was only played to 15. One more point and we would win this sexy volleyball battle.

Carina tossed me the ball, flaunting her tits as she did. Okay, she wasn't flaunting them. I was just obsessed with her ridiculously sexy body.

Casey smacked me on the ass, bringing me back to reality. "Let's go! We've got some Brazilian booties to dominate."

I smiled and scampered back to the end line. I loved Case's enthusiasm during matches. It made me play even harder.

I nailed a jump serve, sending the ball screaming toward Carina. She bumped it to Izzie with no problem. But instead of her tall partner setting it, she decided to go over on two, immediately spiking it.

Casey and I both dove for it, but it hit the sand right between us.

The Brazilians whooped it up as we lay sprawled, our limbs contorted all sexy-like.

Case and I helped each other up and slapped hands. Okay, we blew the first match point, but we weren't giving up.

We went back and forth, both sides almost winning but not quite able to get the two point advantage.

It was 30-29 their advantage. All four of us were panting and sweating. We were totally playing another championship caliber match. Too bad no one was in the stands to see it. Wait, I mean thank God no one was in the stands to see it. Otherwise, they'd see my sweaty, naked body jiggling all over the place. Talk about embarrassing. Fortunately, only my kooky partner and the two hotties across the net were seeing my naughtiness. Though they were going to see me get a lot more naughty if we didn't stop them from winning.

The next point was the most epic of all. A crazy long rally that fans loved watching. Even when the players weren't naked. We battled like warrior princesses (yup, just like Xena - didn't you know she loved playing volleyball?). Nude, sweaty warrior princesses.

It finally ended when Casey and I were totally out of system, and our foes took advantage. Carina hit a sizzling spike to the left side of the court. I scrambled and dove, determined to get there.

The ball bounced off the sand inches from my outstretched hand, giving them the match.

I buried my face and cursed. Which wasn't that smart as I got a mouthful of sand.

Casey knelt next to me, rubbing my back and then helping me up. "Don't worry Leenie. It was an epic match. You were awesome."

I smiled. Somehow she always knew how to take away the sting of defeat. "Thanks Case. You too."

The Brazilians partied on the other side of the net, dancing and shaking their sexy hips.

"American sluts! American sluts!" they chanted, echoing our Brazilian booty cheer from earlier. They thought they were so funny. But they looked hot as hell gyrating all around, so I wasn't complaining about their teasing.

They dashed under the net and almost bowled us over with fierce hugs.

"That was such an awesome match!" Carina exclaimed. "You guys are so good." Her hands roamed down my back until they found my butt, squeezing it firmly.

"Ohhh," I gasped. "Th… thanks. You too. I mean, you and Izzie kick ass." They also grabbed asses crazy good too. Isabella was feeling up Casey while Carina took care of my submissive bottom.

"Ready to be our sex toys?" my lovely dominatrix asked.

I inhaled sharply, realizing this was really happening.

"We're so ready!" Casey shouted. God, that girl was such a nympho. A super-cute nympho who was the best friend and partner in the universe.

Carina's hands moved to the small of my back, pressing into it gently. "Are you sure you're okay with this Alena?"

I stared into her beautiful brown eyes and knew she would never to do anything to hurt me. "Yes. Please make me your slut!"

"Yeah Leenie!" Casey cheered. "That's the spirit."

I blushed, embarrassed that I had confessed my desires so

easily.

Carina seemed to like it. She kissed me. Deep and long. One of those earth-shattering kisses that made me feel like I was floating outside my body and simultaneously feeling her embrace to my core.

When she pulled her lips back, I swayed back and forth, not knowing where I was or even what planet we were on.

"That... that was... wow," I said eloquently.

She gave me that gorgeous smile again. "You're wow *minha fofinha*."

I swooned, but she held me up, pressing her curves along every inch of mine. At that moment, I knew I was going to let this girl do whatever she wanted to me.

Next to us, Casey and Izzie were seeing how far they could stick their tongues down each other's throat.

Carina said something to Izzie in Portuguese, and the statuesque woman tugged Casey and me to the net.

Carina rifled through a bag and scurried back to us holding some rope.

"Oh, w... we're getting tied up?" I asked tentatively.

"Of course. Sex toys should always be bound."

"Oh r... right. Of course." I was new at this sex toy thing. Thank goodness Carina was here to instruct me on how to be a proper slut.

"Yeah Alena, don't you know anything about being a good whore?" Casey teased.

I stuck my tongue out at her. "If I wanted to, I'd just take lessons from you."

Now I was the one getting the tongue stuck at me. We loved poking fun at each other.

Carina seized my ass. "Tonight, Isabella and I will be the only ones giving the lessons, understood?"

"Ohhh God," I moaned from her expert touch. "Y… yes Carina. I'm sorry."

"No need to apologize my sweet Alena. Your body will be the most exquisite temple to explore."

Oh fuck, she made me so wet when she said stuff like that. Like she was some sexy Lara Croft ready to explore my most inner depths.

"Arms over your head gorgeous," she sweetly commanded.

I obeyed as she spun me around, so I was facing the net.

She tied my wrists together and to the net, my bare tits rubbing against the intricately knotted rope.

Izzie tied Casey next to me in a similar position.

My friend grinned at me. "Pretty kinky, huh?"

"Uh… uh huh." I wiggled around, not used to being bound like this. I wasn't used to being bound at all. This was really my first foray into BDSM. I'm glad it was with Casey. I felt better about being a kinky slut as long as she was going to be one alongside me. And I was very glad Carina would be the one administering the sexy punishment.

Our Brazilian captors stepped back, admiring the view.

Isabella commented to Carina in her deep, sensual voice.

"Oh totally," Carina agreed. "These are the two sexiest and sluttiest asses I've ever seen."

A thrill shot through me at hearing that they thought I had a super-sexy ass. But what made it slutty? Oh, maybe the fact that I let Carina tie me up and was wiggling my butt at her. But when she complimented my booty, I felt shaking it for her was what a good sex toy should do.

"Ready to practice our spikes?" the cute Brazilian asked her teammate.

She got an enthusiastic reply, and they scurried off to retrieve some balls.

"Wait, they're going to practice while we're tied up?"

Casey shrugged. "Maybe seeing two hot asses makes them play better."

I nodded. That would certainly explain why they played so ferociously and defeated us.

"Your hot tits and ass definitely motivate me!" Casey continued.

"Casey!"

"What?"

"Stop being ridiculous. Wait, do you really think I'm that hot?"

"Hell yeah! If we weren't best friends, I'd eat your pussy like it was a milkshake." Casey loved milkshakes more than anything, so she was basically saying she'd slurp up my secret sauce like it was the tastiest stuff on earth.

I turned crimson. "Oh my God, would you stop?"

"Well, stop having such a cute pussy."

I must have looked like I had a sunburn. No one could make me blush like this girl.

"You're a total weirdo, you know that?"

"Yup!"

I laughed. Then took in her gorgeous bound body. "Um, y… you have a super-fuckable body too."

"Yes! I knew you wanted to do me."

"Case!"

She giggled. "Oh wait, our sexy captors are back."

Carina and Izzie plopped a bunch of balls on the sand. They stood where we couldn't see them, but I could hear them tossing balls up and down.

Whack! The familiar sound of a palm striking a ball rang out.

Followed by the unfamiliar sound of a ball hitting my ass.

"Ahh!" I cried, surprised by the ass attack.

"Ack!" Casey echoed, struck in her firm butt right after me.

"Hey, what are you guys doing?" I called over my shoulder.

"Practicing," Carina replied. "What better targets than your two lovely asses."

"Hear that Alena, we have the best asses in volleyball!" She wiggled her booty, presenting an even more tempting target.

"Ow!" I yelped as Carina landed another perfect strike. "Great."

The Brazilian duo were uncannily accurate, hitting our reddening asses every time. They were normally precise with their strikes, but they couldn't miss now. I guess our butts were fantastic bullseyes.

Carina varied her speed and placement, making sure to get both my cheeks and testing how much force made them jiggle the most. Okay, so this was what it felt like to be a sex toy. Um, I kinda liked it. Okay, I really liked it.

"Um, Carina, how much longer are you going to practice on our butts?" They weren't hitting the balls as hard as they could, making sure they didn't hurt us. But I was still getting a sore booty.

"Until you realize you're proper sluts."

"Oh we do!" Casey yelled. "We're total volleyball whores!"

"Alena?" Carina asked, tossing a ball in her hand.

"Y… yes. I'm feeling very slutty and helpless."

She didn't reply, but I felt her a moment later, rolling the ball along my ass and down my slit.

She whispered into my ear, coating the ball with my juices. "Your ass is all red, *minha fofinha*."

"That's because some beautiful sexpot keeps hitting it with a volleyball."

"Sexpot?" She moved the ball up and down my lips more rapidly.

"Um, did I mention the beautiful part?" I gasped.

"Yes. You are a very sweet girl. The perfect kind to dominate." She dropped the ball and took both ass cheeks in her hands, squeezing them sinfully and making me go up on my toes.

"Ohh, th… thank you." I was glad my sweetness made me so good at being submissive.

"Fuck Isabella, you're so deep!" Casey screamed beside me. Izzie had her muscular pussy pressed against Casey's equally muscular ass, one arm wrapped around her, fingers buried deep in Casey's cunt.

Oh fuck that was hot. Especially the erotic faces Case was making. Damn, my partner was one sexy gal.

Carina ran her fingers down my slit, making me shiver. "Do you like what they're doing?"

"Oooo, y… yes."

"Would you like me to do that to you?"

"Oh fuck yes!"

She gave my pussy a light spank. "See how good you are at being a slut?"

"Please get inside me Carina. I'll big the biggest slut in the world for you." Wow, she had barely touched me, and I was already willing to do whatever she wanted. Being a sex toy was fun!

She wrapped her arms around me, pressing her breasts and pussy against my back and ass, rubbing her legs against mine. She felt like a velvet blanket that I always wanted touching my skin.

Her left hand found my breast, massaging it softly. While her right slid down my smooth stomach and found my wet mound.

She pierced it gently with two fingers. My body tightened within her grasp, and I moaned softly.

"Mm, Alena, you're so tight," she murmured, probing deeper into me. My body shuddered, flailing beneath her delicate touch.

"That… that feels so good," I moaned.

"How about this?" She curled her fingers upward.

"Ohh fuck! Yes! Right there! Oh my fucking God!"

This woman was a sex goddess. She found the spot that drove me wild instantly, moving her fingers back and forth within my welcoming womanhood.

I thrashed within my bonds, biting onto the rope in the net to stifle my screams.

She grabbed my long hair and tugged my head back. "Uh uh my sweet. I want to hear all your submissive moans."

"S… sorry. I… I'm just so loud."

"The louder the better." She fingered me faster, making my juices run down my legs. And oh boy did I get louder. I moaned, shrieked, and yelled super-slutty things. I really hoped we weren't waking up the neighbors. We were in an open-air stadium after all.

I imagined it full of fans, cheering Carina on as she made me scream, turning me into a complete volleyball slut. Oh fuck, was I turning into a sexy exhibitionist?

Casey was competing with me for biggest slut. She uttered the naughtiest stuff imaginable as Isabella slammed her pussy like a jackhammer. My cute friend's juices were spraying out around Izzie's fingers and coating her thighs. It was one of the hottest things I had ever seen. I would have stared at them all day except I was being driven to a state of delirium by the Brazilian beauty who had taken control of my cunt.

"I want you to cum for me Alena," she told me both sweetly and forcefully.

"Yes! Yes! Please let me cum." I would cum for her all night long with what she was doing to my tender pussy.

She moved her left hand from my nipple to my clit, squeezing it and setting off my floodgates.

"Ohhhhh fuuuccckk!" My body shook violently, and my pussy exploded, squirting out my nectar in a multitude of directions. It covered my thighs, Carina's fingers, and the sand, making the smooth grains look like it had just rained. I had no idea I could squirt this powerfully.

Carina kept rubbing my clit, making me darken a wider and wider circle of sand beneath us.

Casey was doing her damnedest to keep up with me, shooting out impressive glops of sexy cum as Isabella dominated her.

"Scream louder for me," Carina commanded. Izzie gave what I was sure a similar order to Casey.

We both moaned to the heavens and spasmed within our sweet captors' grips, not being able to do anything but spill our sexy sauce. Spill it until they told us we could stop.

They eventually eased up, slowing our orgasms to smaller ones that made us twitch and moan softly.

Carina untied me and lowered me to the sand. I felt like I had no control over my limbs, so I melted into her grasp.

She spooned me, holding me tightly and brushing the sweaty strands out of my face.

Izzie laid Casey nearby, facing me, and wrapped her up in a similar pretzel. We trembled within our lovers' embrace, post-orgasms traveling through our drenched bodies.

"Alena, you look hot as hell," Casey commented, taking in my wet, nude form.

"Y… you too Case. You can really squirt."

"Aw, thanks sweetie. You were a gushing fountain over there."

I blushed and smiled. You knew you had a good friendship

when you could compliment each other on your squirting ability.

Isabella murmured into Casey's ear. She couldn't understand what the powerful Brazilian was saying, but it was having the desired effect. I knew Case well enough to know when she was getting all gooey and crushing on someone. She closed her eyes and let Izzie probe her ear with her agile tongue.

My Brazilian dominatrix ran her fingers over my body, touching me in a way that was both soothing and erotic.

"You look so sexy covered in your own cum."

"Th… thanks." It felt so good being held by her, she could cover me in whatever she wanted.

"May I make love to your gorgeous body again?"

"Oh God yes! Please make love to me all night long."

She laughed, her breath tickling my ear. "As you wish, *minha fofinha*."

I sighed. I didn't know what she kept calling me, but it sounded cute. And, honestly, I loved anything that came out of her mouth.

She found my center again, plunging into my depths like she had been exploring them her whole life. My pussy instantly gave itself over to her, opening all its nooks and crannies and issuing forth its wet gift.

After getting me worked up into a tizzy, she pulled out of me, making my pussy feel like an essential part of it was missing.

"Please don't stop," I begged.

"Don't worry, I'll keep going my sweet. But be a good girl for me and clean my fingers."

She held them to my mouth, dripping with my cum. Oh fuck. No girl had made me taste myself before. But I wanted to be really naughty for Carina.

I opened my lips and sucked on her index finger, licking all my juices off it and feeling like a very dirty slut.

She made me clean all five digits thoroughly and then went back to work, finger banging my needy hole.

She took breaks between her pussy pummeling, sometimes having me clean her fingers, sometimes doing it herself. That was beyond hot, watching her take my most intimate gift into her mouth. And sometimes she just wiped my cum all over my face, reminding me what a whore I was. I had never had any sexual experience like this. But I knew I wanted so many more!

Izzie was also really getting into it, smearing Casey's juices not only on her face but all over her tits and stomach. My best friend was becoming a cum-covered mess. And she had never looked hotter.

Carina and Isabella scooted forward, so Casey and I were closer. Then they took their pussy plunging and clit rubbing up to eleven, making both of us cry out in ecstasy.

"Tell Casey what you want her to do to you," Carina said in that sensual whisper that made it impossible to disobey.

"Ohhhhh fuck! Case, please squirt all over me!" Somehow I knew that's what Carina wanted me to confess. And once I did, I realized how much I really wanted it to happen.

"Alena, please cover me in your juicy cum!" Okay, apparently Casey was just as eager to get more sauce on her.

Our beautiful mistresses made us cum easily, our dual sprays crossing streams and soaking each other. The Brazilians shifted our bodies to make sure we fully coated our partner. I had Case's cum on my legs, tits, stomach, pussy, and face. I licked her essence off my lips. She was both tart and sugary, reflecting her personality perfectly.

Casey was just as covered with my nectar and also gave it a taste, murmuring contentedly and swallowing it. I guess my juices got her stamp of approval. It was awesome having a best friend who gladly lapped up my sweet cum.

Our two sex commanders rolled us in the sand, the soft granules sticking to the cum and making us look like we were getting ready to pose for Cum Sluts Illustrated. A magazine I would totally buy if it existed. Wait, did it exist? I needed to do some research online after this. Though starring in our own version of it was even better!

I reached out to Casey, and she took my hand.

"Doing okay Leenie?"

"Yeah. You?"

"Oh yeah. I'm totally covered in your delicious cum!"

I giggled. Only she could make that sound like the most amazing thing in the world. "Me too. I mean, in your tasty cum. Well, mine and yours. Fuck, I have a lot of cum on me."

"As well you should," Carina informed me. "Sex toys should be constantly drenched in it."

"Can I be drenched in your cum?" I asked hopefully.

She smiled and squeezed me. "Of course. You are a very quick study in being a slut Alena."

"Oh I always knew there was a wonder whore inside Miss Goody Two Shoes."

"Hey!"

"Own it Alena! Wonder Whore - battling the forces of evil with her tight pussy, perky tits, and super-jiggly butt!"

We all laughed, imagining that scenario. Izzie joining in after a quick translation from Carina.

"Okay, okay," I said after I got my giggling fit under control. "Wonder Whore really needs to lick your beautiful pussy Carina."

"Patience my darling slut. First we must get you two properly submissive."

"Um, haven't we been really submissive?" Case and I had let

them do whatever they wanted to us. But I guess there were levels of submissiveness beyond that. I had so much to learn.

They got more rope (these girls really came prepared) and bound our arms behind us in L-shapes. Then tied our thighs and ankles together.

Casey and I knelt on our haunches, barely able to move, our bare legs rubbing against each other.

"You guys are so good at this," Casey gushed.

I nodded rapidly in agreement. Carina and Isabella were expert volleyball players. But even more expert at dominating sexy sluts.

"You two are going to go down on us and drink all our cum," Carina commanded.

Casey and I nodded, eager to taste their beautiful Brazilian pussies and show them how submissive we could be.

"But first, you need to be put in the right mood."

"We are totally in the right mood!" I shouted.

Casey giggled, bumping me with her hip. "I am totally rubbing off on you."

I bit my lip. That was something she would say. Fuck, these three were really making me lose my inhibitions.

Carina took my cheeks and kissed me. "I love your enthusiasm my sweet Alena. But trust me, this will make you extra slutty."

I nodded, very much wanting to be extra slutty.

She spoke quickly to Izzie, who got a huge smile and scampered off, returning quickly with two big dildos.

My eyes went wide. How much kinky stuff did these two bring with them? And did they always travel with this stuff? Did they fuck each other at each stop on the tour or just dominate willing sluts like us? I needed all those questions answered. After I had my hole stuffed and ate out Carina's gorgeous pussy.

"We're going to stick these deep in your slut holes."

I shuddered. "But... th... they're so big."

"So fucking big." Casey was fixated on the sex toys, her face a mixture of excitement and trepidation. I totally understood how she felt.

Isabella rubbed Casey's back and kissed her on the cheek, obviously trying to soothe her. What sweethearts she and Carina were. Sweethearts who totally owned our pussies.

Carina nestled her body against mine, stroking my arms and legs. "Don't worry. We'll go nice and slow. And show you exactly how much of a whore you both can be."

I looked at Casey. We nodded at each other. There was just something about these two that made it impossible to refuse them. It probably had to do with all the epic orgasms they kept making us have. They were so cool that way!

They bent us forward, gently laying our heads on the sand, keeping us on our knees with our butts sticking up. Well, this was definitely a submissive position to be fucked in.

Carina plucked the purple dildo from Isabella's hand, leaving the blue one for her. Man, how did Carina know purple was one of my favorite colors? Maybe she was a pussy psychic: the more she plundered a woman's tenderness, the more she knew about her. What a great power!

Casey's cute face was right next to mine. "I'm so glad you're getting fucked next to me."

I smiled. She was so adorable. "Me too Case. There's no one I'd rather be a big slut with. Um, you know what I mean."

"Totally!" Her big grin turned to one of painful pleasure as Izzie pierced her lips. "Holy shit!!"

Carina immediately followed suit, pressing the behemoth against my tightness and making my lips part for it.

"Ohhh Goddd!" I had never had something so large in me before. It's not that I didn't like playing with vibrators. I just had smaller ones.

Carina rubbed my butt. "You're doing great my sweet."

I groaned in response, not able to get any coherent words out. She slid it in farther. My eyes watered, trying to withstand the blissful torture.

The Brazilians chatted with each other as they slowly worked the fake cocks into us.

"Isabella agrees you both have wonderfully tight pussies."

"Ohhh fuck, thank you!" I groaned.

"Oh God, shove them in farther!" Casey pleaded.

The purple and blue fuck toys went in all the way, making us both gasp and almost forget how to breath. We whimpered and moaned, our pussies pulsating around the devastating dildos, our limbs pulling uselessly against the tight ropes binding us. Okay, now I totally knew what it felt like to be a sex toy. I was completely helpless with my pussy totally gorged and about to pleasure a Brazilian goddess. And I had never been so turned on in my life.

Casey smiled through her cute cries and groans, obviously loving it as much as me.

"Mmm," Carina commented. "Your pussies and asses look so hot from this angle, especially with those huge cocks filling you."

Casey and I could only moan in response.

"Now for the real fun." The vibrators began rumbling within us, sending our cries to a whole other level.

"Oh my..."

"Fucking God!" Casey finished for me.

Before we could get any more erotic screams out, Carina and Izzie plopped their cute butts in front of us, laid back, and grabbed our hair, depositing our mouths on their beautiful pussies.

I immediately slipped my tongue inside her, tasting her wonderful tightness. Her salty sweetness hugged my tongue, pulling it in and inviting it to stay for as long as it liked. Well, as long as she liked really. She had a firm grip on my hair and was holding me to her mound. I wasn't going anywhere until I had pleasured her to her satisfaction. I was totally fine with that. I could stay nose down in this pussy forever.

Casey slurped up Izzie's folds, putting her all into it. Oh, that little sneak wasn't going to beat me. I plunged deep into Carina and swirled my tongue around, probing for the spots that made her writhe and moan the most.

"Uhhhh Alena! Yes! Yes my sweet slut! Right there!" Okay, I guess I found it. I attacked her tenderness and got her bucking like a Brazilian bronco, both hands sifting through my lush hair, refusing to let me move from between her supple thighs.

My own juices were leaking down my legs, the sinful vibrations from the cock monster inside me making me convulse and moan into Carina's lips. With my thighs bound so tightly, the dildo was absolutely destroying my pussy. In the best way possible.

I knew Carina was about to blow, so I moved to her clit. It was so cute, sticking out of its hood, waiting for me to attend to it. I flicked it with my tongue, making Carina's whole body tremble. I ran circles around it and sucked on it, driving her into a wild frenzy. I loved giving her so much pleasure, her sensual cries inspiring me to never let go of her lovely nub.

"Oh *porra*! I'm cumming! I'm cumming!" Boy did she. An explosion of cum erupted out of her juicy pussy, flowing down my throat and splattering my face. She held my head between her legs, making sure I lapped it all up. I was happy to do it, tasting her sweetness on my tongue and lips.

She gyrated her hips, smearing her pussy juice all over my face. God, this girl really knew how to make me feel like a total whore.

When she was finally done, she lifted my head and kissed me savagely, tasting herself on my lips. She held my bound body, and I knew I was completely hers.

Casey's cute face was just as much of a mess, just with Izzie's lovely cum. She had a goofy grin on her face, obviously having loved going down on her muscular mistress.

The Brazilian duo scooted Casey and me next to each other, readjusting the vibrators so they were as deep as possible in us.

"Kiss each other," Carina commanded.

I looked at Casey. Oh shit, kiss my best friend? Could I do… nevermind. Casey plastered her lips against mine, not giving me time to think about it. They were soft and pliable, and I instantly merged mine with hers. I tasted Casey's saliva and Izzie's cum, and Casey was obviously getting a sample of Carina's juices from my mouth. In a way, it was like all four of us were making out. It was lovely.

Carina and Isabella went back and forth, making us eat them out and having us kiss them or each other. I got to taste Izzie's delectable pussy as well as more of Carina's. So now I had four flavors of cum on me, including my own. The Brazilians had kept their promise of making us feel like complete sex toys.

For their next trick, they kept us bound and bent over, placing us side by side, my right thigh touching Casey's left.

They used the big dildos as strap-ons, fucking our sore pussies hard. Carina took care of mine while Izzie handled Casey's. The sounds of their hips slapping against our asses reverberated through the arena. As did our sensual moans.

Casey's face was inches from mine. Her breath hot on my face as unintelligible noises escaped her lips. She looked hot as hell. I hoped I did too as I cried out submissively.

"Tell us what you are," Carina ordered, Izzie repeating it in Portuguese. Or at least I assumed that's what she said. Whatever it was, it brooked no defiance.

"We're your sex toys! Our bodies belong to you!" Casey and I said in unison. Wow, we really were best friends: we said the exact same thing when we were being super-sluts.

They rubbed our butts. "You girls really are the best." I smiled through my moaning. Yes, I loved being the best slut.

Carina's finger moved to my tiniest hole. Oh fuck, was she going to… uhhhhhh! Fuck, she did. Her fingertip pierced my ass, coated in my juices. That made it slide in easier but fuck it barely fit. I had never had anything in my butt before. It felt weird, a little painful, but also kinda nice.

"You okay *minha fofinha*?"

"Ohhhh, y… yeah."

"Do you want me to keep going?"

"Y… yes please." Now that she had penetrated my virgin ass, I wanted to see how much I could take. If I was going to be a slut, I might as well add ass whore to my resume.

I winced as she worked it in farther. God I was so fucking tight. My ass clenched her finger powerfully, so it felt like the huge purple dildo was entering me.

I blinked my eyes open and saw just from Casey's face that she was getting anally probed too. She panted and begged for more.

Somehow Carina got her finger all the way into me. And then gave me a double fucking, plundering my pussy with her fake cock and pillaging my ass with her finger. Fuck, it felt amazing. It was my first time getting fucked in both holes at once, my first anal period. But it wasn't going to be my last. She was opening me to a whole world of sexual experiences. I was very grateful. I'd have to show my appreciation by eating out her tasty pussy whenever she wanted.

Somehow the anal probing made my orgasms even more amazing than before, which I didn't think was possible. I squirted out a steady stream, drenching Carina's stomach and pussy and shrieking into the sand.

She kept pummeling me, my two holes engorged beyond belief. And I kept cumming. And screaming. And telling Carina whatever slutty thing she wanted me to confess.

When I thought I was done and her finger popped free, another one replaced it. A stronger, longer one. Oh shit, it was Izzie's finger. They were fingering their partner's whore while still fucking their favorite plaything. That set off a whole other round of climaxing, Izzie's finger expanding my poor ass even more than Carina's. I was glad Carina had softened me up first. But felt bad for Casey, who got the larger finger first. Though I hadn't heard any complaints. Just grunts and groans of submissive joy.

After fucking us a bunch more, they let us collapse into the sand. I was nestled against Casey, our chests' heaving, our bound bodies trembling from the mini-orgasms that were still leaking out of us.

Apparently we didn't look enough like sex slaves, since the dominating Brazilians fingered their tight pussies and rubbed their sensitive clits, spraying their seed all over us. Casey and I took it. We didn't really have much choice. We were totally tied up and still shaking from the ultra-fucking they had given us.

Carina and Izzie finished and fell on top of us. They untied us and we wound up in a pretzel of warm, cum-covered sand. It felt wonderful, so many soft and firm nude bodies touching me.

No one said anything. We just touched each other gently, enjoying the tender snuggling.

The girls finally had to leave. They had a plane to catch in the morning. We shared lots of hugs, kisses and pats on the ass.

Carina gave me a particularly deep kiss and ass squeeze. "See you in Brasil *minha fofinha*. Where we'll really have fun."

I clutched her like I never wanted her to leave. So wait? Was what we just did a warm-up? What exactly did they plan to do to us in two weeks at the next tournament? I couldn't wait to find out!

As a parting gift, they pinched our clits, somehow setting off a tidal wave of orgasms in both me and Casey.

"*Ate breve meninas,*" Isabella called over her shoulder.

"See you soon girls," Carina translated.

Casey and I fell to the sand, holding each other as we came and watched two beautiful Brazilian butts swish back and forth.

We came long after they had left the stadium, grinding our pussies against our partner's thigh, hip, and whatever other body part was nearby.

"Oh fuck Case, I'm cumming all over you!"

"That's what best friends do!"

"Ahhh it feels so good! But, um, most best friends don't do that."

"God I can't stop! That's what makes us the best friends in the universe!"

I laughed through my passionate throes. I loved this girl so much.

"Yes! Yes! You're totally right. I want to keep cumming on you forever!"

"Soak me you little slut!"

We soaked each other good, leaving our bodies a wet, sticky mess.

When our pussies finally settled down, I buried my face in her shoulder, still trembling. "Can... can you hold me for a little while?"

"I got ya Leenie." She wrapped her arms around me, and I snuggled into her warm cocoon.

***

Back at the hotel, we thoroughly showered, getting all the layers of cum off us. We wound up bathing together. We had been naked and fuck toys around each other the whole night, so it's not like showering together was weird. I certainly had seen Casey naked plenty of times when we changed for matches. But tonight I had seen so much more of her. And I kinda liked it.

We changed into comfy sleep shorts and T-shirts and hopped into our beds.

I bit my lip, staring at my bestie.

"What's up?" she asked.

"Um, would it be okay if I…"

"Get your cute butt over here!"

I grinned. She knew me so well. I jumped out of bed and slid under the covers next to her, taking her hand.

She beamed at me, all goofy-like.

"What?"

"I was just thinking, in one day we won our first championship and got dominated by the hottest Brazilian girls on the planet."

I smiled. "So, best day ever?"

She squeezed my hand. "Definitely best day ever."

Her mouth curled into one of her mischievous grins. "And we got to find out what a crazy vocal slut you are."

"Casey!" I pinched her side, then covered my face in my hands, remembering all my whorish confessions.

"Oh God, I can't believe I said all those things."

She pulled my hands down, rubbing them gently. "I'm glad you did. It made me feel better not being the only super-slutty one!"

Her smile was contagious. "Oh, well, okay. So… maybe I

should keep doing that when Carina and Izzie fuck us next time?"

"Oh you should definitely keep doing that. You're hot as hell!"

I blushed. "Case, you're one sexy weirdo."

"Thank you!"

I rubbed her shoulder. "And one amazing best friend."

She beamed at me. "Aw, you too Leenie. Now turn over and stick that hot ass against my pussy."

She flipped me onto my other side before I could protest and wrapped her arms and legs around me. She was super-cozy, and I instantly relaxed into her, letting my body meld with hers.

"You're a good snuggler," I cooed contentedly.

"And you're one sexy pillow!"

I giggled, tracing my fingers down her arm. "What do you think the girls have planned for us in Brazil?"

She clutched me tightly. "The most epic, submissive sexual shenanigans ever! Get ready to open the floodgates of that adorable pussy of yours!"

My cheeks burned crimson. Oh my God, Casey was so freakin' graphic. Though it was nice she thought my pussy was adorable. And I was getting hot thinking about turning my body over to our Brazilian lovers again.

"Sounds wonderful," I sighed, snuggling into Casey and closing my eyes.

Her gentle breath tickled my hair as she buried her face in my long locks. I dozed off, dreaming of exciting tournaments and sinful sex.

It was going to be one amazing summer on tour.

More Fun and Sexy Books by Riley Rose

Supernatural Submission Series
Elena Cortez loves Halloween. So when her new sexy neighbor Cassia invites her to a Halloween party, she's super-stoked! Only problem: Elena thinks Cassia might be a witch. Like a real witch. Who's using her magic to make Elena have the most epic orgasms of her life! Even better? Elena suspects her other new neighbor, Juliana, is a super-sexy vampire who wants to bite her soft, submissive flesh. Will Elena let Cassia and Juliana have their supernatural way with her? Find out in this fun, Halloween-themed erotica!

The Mara and KATT Sex Chronicles
Mara Keoni is a sexy Navajo special agent of the Independent Justice Foundation. But she never expected to be paired with KATT, an incredibly advanced female AI inside a sports car. Not only is KATT very eager to help Mara on her missions, but she's also eager to pleasure Mara in every way possible with her many "enhancements." Will Mara succumb to her curiosity and find out exactly what KATT can do to her? Find out in Submitting to My Robot Car and Seduced by My Robot Car - Books 1 and 2 of The Mara and KATT Sex Chronicles!

Laia Rios: Sex Raider Series
Laia Rios is the most amazing adventurer and relic hunter on the planet. When she gets word of a new clue to the legendary Lust Idol of the Amazons, she can't pass up the opportunity to find it. And all she'll have to do is pass through a temple filled with the most elaborate sex traps ever and submit her body to a bunch of Amazons with the most amazing bodies on the planet. Will Laia be able to withstand all the Amazons' physical and sexual tests?

Find out if the Sex Raider is up for the challenge in this sexy and fun action/adventure erotic series!

Submissive MILF Series
Alex Masters is the hottest MILF in town! And her daughter's best friend Melody knows it. After crushing on Alex for years, Melody finally decides to make her move on Alex's sexy and sultry body. Will Alex let herself be seduced by her daughter's super-cute and sexy 20 year-old friend? Will she let Melody pleasure her in extremely kinky ways? And will she become the most submissive and sexy MILF on the planet? Find out how naughty this hot mom can get!

Visit RileyRoseErotica.com to get a Free eBook and learn more about Riley's books and the Decadent Fantasy Universe!

E-mail: Riley@RileyRoseErotica.com

Facebook: RileyRoseErotica
Twitter: @RileyRoserotica
Instagram: @RileyRoseErotica

About the Author

Riley Rose loves writing fun and adventurous erotic fiction set in the action, sci-fi, and fantasy genres, focusing on stories with heart, humor, and characters who keep losing their clothes. Riley is working on a shared universe of erotica, the Decadent Fantasy Universe, where characters from different series and stories will crossover with each other. Blending action, humor, and sexy shenanigans, Riley brings a unique blend of sweet and sexy stories featuring fun-loving characters, whose adventures you'll hopefully want to follow for a long time. Find out more at RileyRoseErotica.com.

Printed in Great Britain
by Amazon